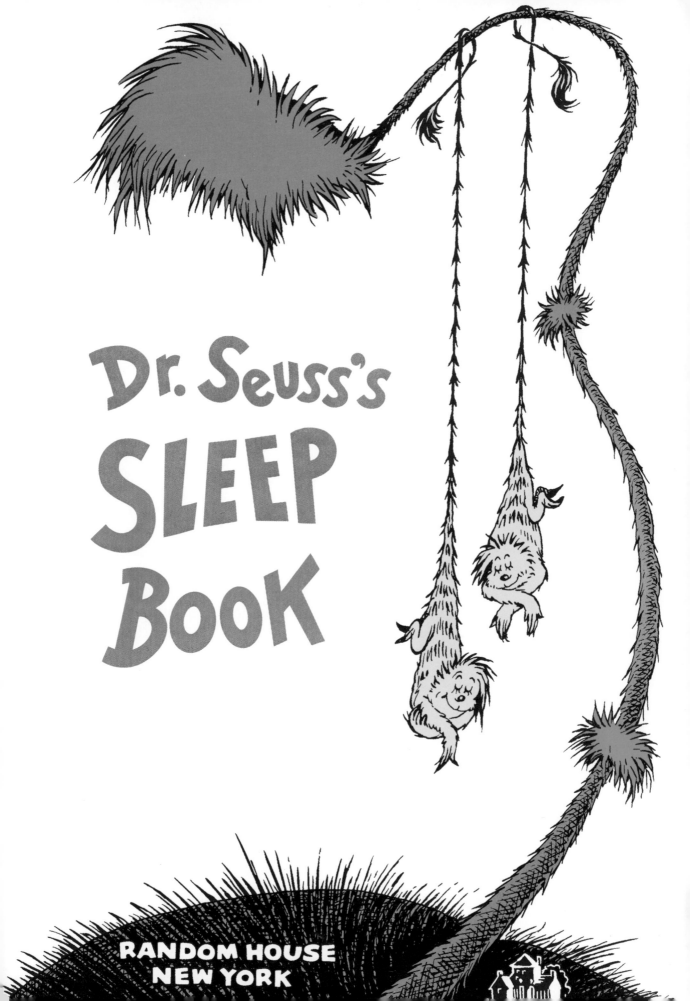

Dr. Seuss's SLEEP BOOK

RANDOM HOUSE
NEW YORK

For Marie and Bert Hupp

TM & copyright © by Dr. Seuss Enterprises, L.P. 1962, copyright renewed 1990

All rights reserved.
Published in the United States by Random House Children's Books,
a division of Random House, Inc., New York.

Random House and the colophon are registered trademarks of Random House, Inc.

Visit us on the Web!
randomhouse.com/kids
Seussville.com
Kohls.com/Cares

Educators and librarians, for a variety of teaching tools, visit us at
RHTeachersLibrarians.com

This special edition was printed for Kohl's Department Stores, Inc.
(for distribution on behalf of Kohl's Cares, LLC, its wholly owned subsidiary)
by Random House Children's Books, a division of Random House, Inc., New York.

Kohl's
ISBN: 978-0-375-97278-2
123386
09/12–02/13

MANUFACTURED IN CHINA

10 9 8 7 6 5 4 3 2 1

The news

Just came in
From the County of Keck
That a very small bug
By the name of Van Vleck
Is yawning so wide
You can look down his neck.

This may not seem
Very important, I know.
But it *is*. So I'm bothering
Telling you so.

A yawn is quite catching, you see. Like a cough.
It just takes one yawn to start other yawns off.
NOW the news has come in that some friends of Van Vleck's
Are yawning so wide you can look down *their* necks.

At this moment, right now,
Under seven more noses,
Great yawns are in blossom.
They're blooming like roses.

The yawn of that one little bug is still spreading!
According to latest reports, it is heading
Across the wide fields, through the sleepy night air,
Across the whole country toward every-which-where.
And people are gradually starting to say,
"I feel rather drowsy. I've had quite a day."

Creatures are starting to think about rest.

Two Biffer-Baum Birds are now building their nest.

They do it each night. And quite often I wonder

How they do this big job without making a blunder.

But that is *their* problem.

Not yours. And not mine.

The point is: They're going to bed.

And that's fine.

Sleep thoughts

Are spreading

Throughout the whole land.

The time for night-brushing of teeth is at hand.

Up at Herk-Heimer Falls, where the great river rushes

And crashes down crags in great gargling gushes,

The Herk-Heimer Sisters are using their brushes.

Those falls are just grand for tooth-brushing beneath

If you happen to be up that way with your teeth.

The news just came in from the Castle of Krupp
That the lights are all out and the drawbridge is up.
And the old drawbridge draw-er just said with a yawn,
"My drawbridge is drawn and it's going to stay drawn
'Til the milkman delivers the milk, about dawn.
I'm going to bed now. So nobody better
Come round with a special delivery letter."

The number
Of sleepers
Is steadily growing.
Bed is where
More and more people are going.
In Culpepper Springs, in the Stilt-Walkers' Hall,
The stilt-walkers' stilts are all stacked on the wall.
The stilt-walker walkers have called it a day.
They're all tuckered out and they're snoozing away.
This is very big news. It's important to know.
And that's why I'm bothering telling you so.

Way out in the west, in the town of Mercedd,
The Hinkle-Horn Honking Club just went to bed.
Every horn has been quietly hung on a hook,
For the night, in its own private Hinkle-Horn Nook.

All this long, happy day, they've been honking about
And the Hinkle-Horn Honkers have honked themselves out.
But they'll wake up quite fresh in the morning. And then . . .
They'll start right in Hinkle-Horn honking again.

Everywhere, creatures
Are falling asleep.
The Collapsible Frink
Just collapsed in a heap.
And, by adding the Frink
To the others before,
I am able to give you
The Who's-Asleep-Score:
Right now, forty thousand
Four hundred and four
Creatures are happily,
Deeply in slumber.
I think you'll agree
That's a whopping fine number.

Counting up sleepers . . ?

Just how do we do it . . ?

Really quite simple. There's nothing much to it.

We find out how many, we learn the amount

By an Audio-Telly-o-Tally-o Count.

On a mountain, halfway between Reno and Rome,

We have a machine in a plexiglass dome

Which listens and looks into everyone's home.

And whenever it sees a new sleeper go flop,

It jiggles and lets a new Biggel-Ball drop.

Our chap counts these balls as they plup in a cup.

And that's how we know who is down and who's up.

KEEP OUT

Do you talk in your sleep . . ?

It's a wonderful sport

And I have some news of this sport to report.

The World-Champion Sleep-Talkers, Jo and Mo Redd-Zoff,

Have just gone to sleep and they're talking their heads off.

For fifty-five years, now, each chattering brother

Has babbled and gabbled all night to the other.

They've talked about laws and they've talked about gauze.
They've talked about paws and they've talked about flaws.
They've talked quite a lot about old Santa Claus.
And the reason I'm telling you this is because
You should take up this sport. It's just fine for the jaws.

Do you walk in your sleep . . ?

I just had a report

Of some interesting news of this popular sport.

Near Finnigan Fen, there's a sleepwalking group

Which not only walks, but it walks a-la-hoop!

Every night they go miles. Why, they walk to such length

They have to keep eating to keep up their strength.

So, every so often, one puts down his hoop,
Stops hooping and does some quick snooping for soup.
That's why they are known as the Hoop-Soup-Snoop Group.

Sleepwalking, too, are the Curious Crandalls

Who sleepwalk on hills with assorted-sized candles.

The Crandalls walk nightly in slumbering peace

In spite of slight burns from the hot dripping grease.

The Crandalls wear candles because they walk far

And, if they wake up,

Want to see where they are.

Now the news has arrived
From the Valley of Vail
That a Chippendale Mupp has just bitten his tail,
Which he does every night before shutting his eyes.
Such nipping sounds silly. But, really, it's wise.

He has no alarm clock. So this is the way

He makes sure that he'll wake at the right time of day.

His tail is so long, he won't feel any pain

'Til the nip makes the trip and gets up to his brain.

In exactly eight hours, the Chippendale Mupp

Will, at last, feel the bite and yell "Ouch!" and wake up.

A Mr. and Mrs. J. Carmichael Krox
Have just gone to bed near the town of Fort Knox.
And they, by the way, have the finest of clocks.

I'm not at all sure that I quite quite understand
Just how the thing works, with that one extra hand.
But I *do* know this clock does one very slick trick.
It doesn't tick tock. How it goes, is tock tick.
So, with ticks in its tocker, and tocks in its ticker
It saves lots of time and the sleepers sleep quicker.

What a fine night for sleeping! From all that I hear,
It's the best night for sleeping in many a year.
They're even asleep in the Zwieback Motel!
And people don't usually sleep there too well.

The beds are like rocks and, as everyone knows,
The sheets are too short. They won't cover your toes.
SO, if people are actually sleeping in THERE . . .
It's a great night for sleeping! It must be the air.

It's a great night for snores! I just had a report
Of some boys who are tops in this musical sport.
The snortiest snorers in all our fair land
Are Snorter McPhail and his Snore-a-Snort Band.
This band can snore *Dixie* and old *Swanee River*
So loud it would make forty elephants shiver.

The loudest of all of the boys is McPhail.

HE snores with his head in a three-gallon pail.

So they snore in a cave twenty miles out of town.

If they snored closer in, they would snore the town down.

Do you know who's asleep
Out in Foona-Lagoona . . ?
Two very nice
Foona-Lagoona Baboona.

We've added them into our Who's-Asleep Count
Which has grown to a really amazing amount.
Exactly eight million, eight hundred and eight
Creatures are sleeping now! Isn't that great!

A Jedd is in bed,

And the bed of a Jedd

Is the softest

Of beds in the world,

It is said.

He makes it from pom poms

He grows on his head.

And he's sleeping right now

On the softest of fluff,

Completely exhausted

From growing the stuff.

The news has come in from the District of Dofft
That two Offt are asleep and they're sleeping aloft.
And how are they able to sleep off the ground . . ?
I'll tell you. I weighed one last week and I found
That an Offt is SO light he weighs minus one pound!

A moose is asleep.

He is dreaming of moose drinks.

A goose is asleep.

He is dreaming of goose drinks.

That's well and good when a moose dreams of moose juice.

And nothing goes wrong when a goose dreams of goose juice.

But it isn't too good when a moose and a goose

Start dreaming they're drinking the other one's juice.

Moose juice, not goose juice, is juice for a moose

And goose juice, not moose juice, is juice for a goose.

So, when goose gets a mouthful of juices of moose's

And moose gets a mouthful of juices of goose's,

They always fall out of their beds screaming screams.

SO . . .

I'm warning you, now! Never drink in your dreams.

Speaking of dreaming,

I think you should note

That the Bumble-Tub Club is now dreaming afloat.

Every night they go dreaming down Bumble-Tub Creek

Except for one night, every third or fourth week,

When they stop for repairs. 'Cause their bumble-tubs leak.

But tonight they're afloat, full of dreams, full of bliss,

And that's why I'm bothering telling you this.

At the fork of a road

In the Vale of Va-Vode

Five foot-weary salesmen have laid down their load.

All day they've raced round in the heat, at top speeds,

Unsuccessfully trying to sell Zizzer-Zoof Seeds

Which nobody wants because nobody needs.

Tomorrow will come. They'll go back to their chore.
They'll start on the road, Zizzer-Zoofing once more
But tonight they've forgotten their feet are so sore.
And that's what the wonderful night time is for.

Everywhere,
Creatures
Have shut off their voices.
They've all gone to bed
In the beds of their choices.

They're sleeping in bushes. They're sleeping in crannies.
Some on their stomachs, and some on their fannies.
They're peacefully sleeping in comfortable holes.
Some, even, on soft-tufted barber shop poles.
The number of sleepers is now past the millions!
The number of sleepers is now in the billions!

They're sleeping on steps! And on strings! And on floors!

In mailboxes, ships, and the keyholes of doors!

Every worm on a fishhook is safe for the night.

Every fish in the sea is too sleepy to bite.

Every whale in the ocean has turned off his spout.

Every light between here and Far Foodle is out.

And now, adding things up, we are way beyond billions!

Our Who's-Asleep-Score is now up in the Zillions!

Ninety-nine zillion,
Nine trillion and two
Creatures are sleeping!
So . . .
How about you?

When you put out *your* light,
Then the number will be
Ninety-nine zillion
Nine trillion and three.

Good night.